LUCKIEST MATILDA

Written by Tracy Andersen

Illustrated by Zachery Manza

Story by Tracy Andersen
Cover and Interior Illustrations
by Zachery Manza
Copyright 2021, Tracy Andersen

Photo of Matilda courtesy of
Tracy Voss with TracysPawsRecuse

ISBN : 978 - 0 - 578 - 30811 - 1

For all those beautiful people who dedicate their lives to rescue those who have no voice.

Matilda sat in a Texas shelter all alone,
hoping someone would take her home.

She patiently waited everyday
for that family to come her way.

Then it happened in September, a day Matilda will always remember. The window down and the wind in her ears, her eyes filled with happy tears.

A crowd greeted her when she arrived, dogs of every shape and size. Many days they played outside until it was time for another ride.

Meanwhile 2000 miles away, a family hoped and prayed to find a dog to call their own and welcome to their happy home.

Just one picture was all it took,
the family knew that they were hooked.

In the bus the dogs did climb,

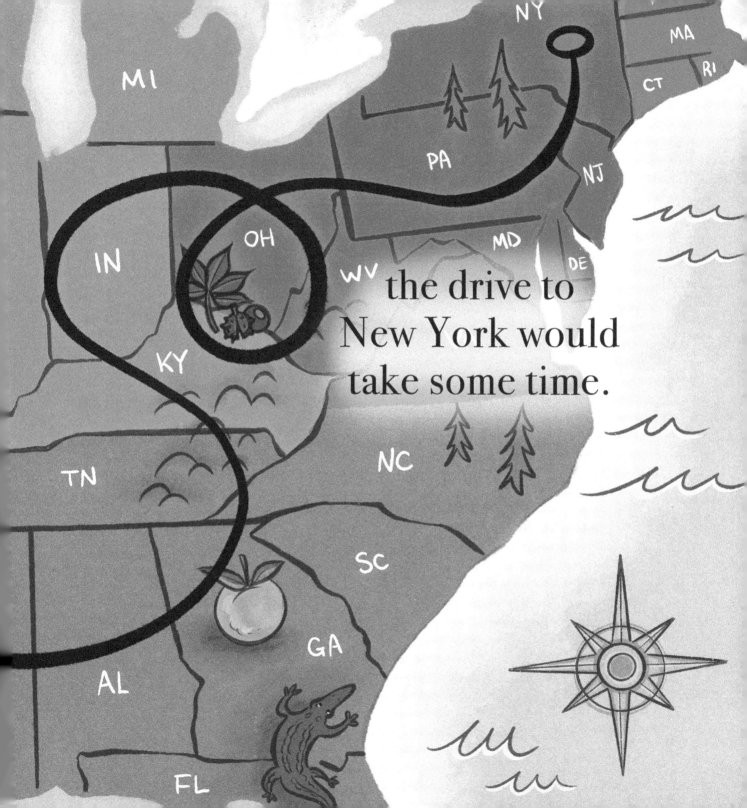

the drive to
New York would
take some time.

Families gathered from far and near
to greet the bus with a cheer.

And through the crowd they heard her name,

the woman from the bus exclaimed.

In their arms she was placed,
nothing but love upon their face.

Sure Matilda was a lucky dog....
But it was her family who
was luckiest of all.

THE END

Matilda was rescued and adopted in 2017.
She is currently living her best life
in upstate New York.

CPSIA information can be obtained
at www.ICGtesting.com
Printed in the USA
LVHW070801100122
708164LV00007B/117